THE·LAND·OF
NOD

THE BLACK MOUNTAIN

THE FLOATING ISLES

SNOWY VILLAGE

ENCHANTED VALLEY

CREEPY CASTLE

GLOOMY DEN

GLITTER BAY

BOULDER GORGE

N
W   E
S

THE
ANCIENT FOREST

OUTER
SPACE

EMERALD GLEN

GIANTS' TOWN

DEADLY
CREEK

RICKETY
BRIDGE

THE
STINKY
SWAMPS

GOLDEN
COVE

For Lara: spread your wings and believe!
R.F.

LADYBIRD BOOKS

UK | USA | Canada | Ireland | Australia | India | New Zealand | South Africa

Ladybird Books is part of the Penguin Random House group of companies
whose addresses can be found at global.penguinrandomhouse.com.

www.penguin.co.uk   www.puffin.co.uk   www.ladybird.co.uk

Penguin
Random House
UK

First published 2022
001

Written by Rhiannon Fielding. Text copyright © Ladybird Books Ltd, 2022
Illustrations copyright © Chris Chatterton, 2022
Moral rights asserted

Printed in Italy

The authorized representative in the EEA is Penguin Random House Ireland,
Morrison Chambers, 32 Nassau Street, Dublin D02 YH68

A CIP catalogue record for this book is available from the British Library
ISBN: 978–0–241–54559–1
All correspondence to:
Ladybird Books, Penguin Random House Children's
One Embassy Gardens, 8 Viaduct Gardens London SW11 7BW

TEN MINUTES TO BED

Little Fairy

Rhiannon Fielding • Chris Chatterton

In a **magical glade** near a sparkling stream,
where the soft mossy ground is **velvety green**,
a **delicate call** could be heard overhead:

"Come on, little fairies . . .
ten minutes to bed!"

On **elegant wings,** which were graceful and bright,
the fairies flew round in the **warm evening light.**
Nine minutes to bedtime – they fluttered around . . .

but **one little fairy** remained near the ground.

Her **wings** were
so little that,
   try as she might . . .

Poppy could **never quite**
reach the same height.

"Eight minutes to bed!"
said her mum with relief.

But Poppy, determined,
jumped on to a leaf.

She **didn't** feel graceful –
just clumsy
and small.

She didn't feel much
like a **fairy** at all!

Seven minutes to bed –

there was still time to try . . .

Poppy opened her wings,
and she **willed** them to fly.

A spark
and a quiver . . .

a quick burst of
power!

She landed with joy on a tall purple flower.
"Six minutes to bed!" came the call from below,

but Poppy
was watching the
fireflies glow.

As she made her way upwards,
her **confidence** grew,

and she **laughed** as she passed
other creatures she knew.

Five minutes –
she'd never flown up quite so high!
From here, all around,
she could see the
night sky.

Just then, Poppy heard a **mysterious** sound –
a strange sort of **grumbling**, down on the ground!

With a leap, then a *whoosh*,
feeling no longer scared,
she **swiftly** flew downwards
as **fast** as she dared.

Quick as an arrow, she landed, unfazed –

from the trees other fairies were watching, amazed!

On the ground was a gnome, with his face growing red:

"I'm lost, and it's only
four minutes to bed!"

Under the **dark sky** and **far from his glade,**
the **lost, worried gnome** felt a little afraid.

Three minutes to bed . . .

Poppy had an idea!

"I'll help you
get home –
I can stay nice
and near!"

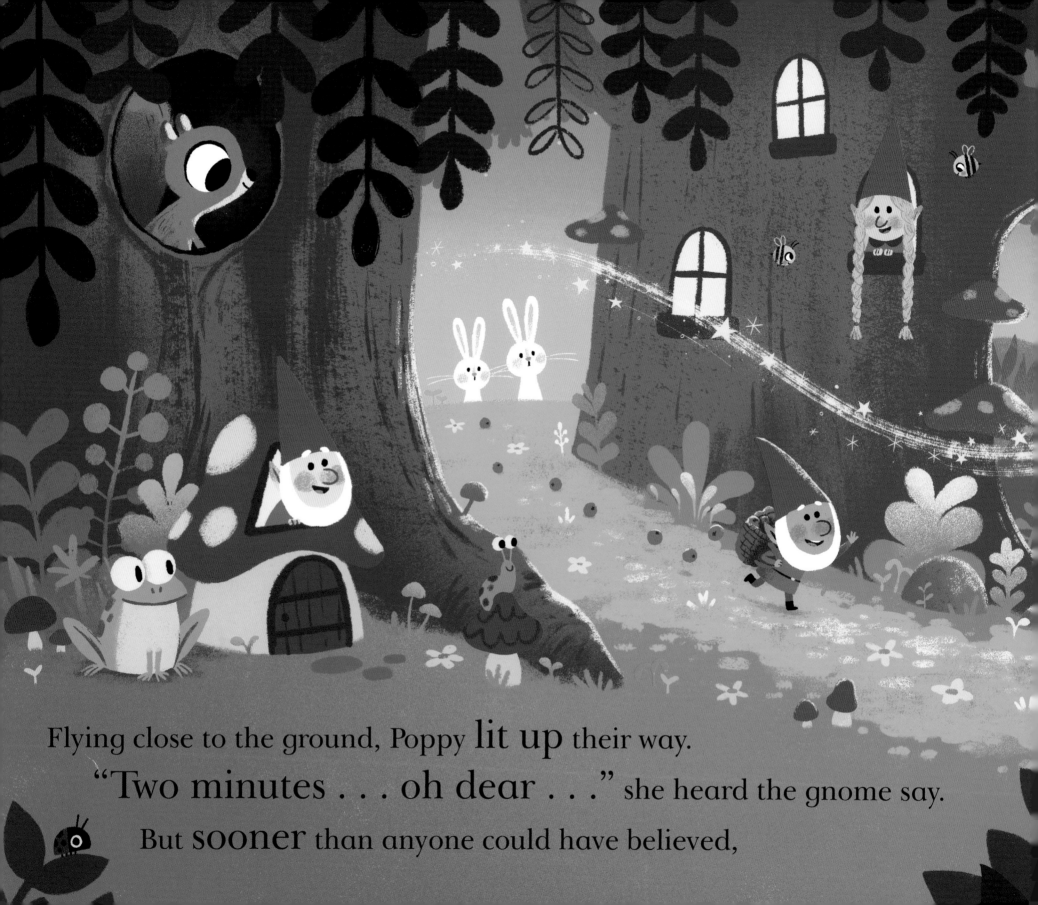

Flying close to the ground, Poppy lit up their way.

"Two minutes . . . oh dear . . ." she heard the gnome say.

But sooner than anyone could have believed,

her new friend was home,
feeling very relieved.

Soon, Poppy saw some soft lights overhead.

"Well done!" said her mummy. "One minute to bed."

Poppy folded her wings with a yawn – time to rest . . .

Flying high wasn't bad,
but down here was the best!

THE · LAND · OF
NOD

THE
BLACK
MOUNTAIN

THE
FLOATING
ISLES

SNOWY
VILLAGE

ENCHANTED
VALLEY

CREEPY
CASTLE

GLOOMY
DEN

BOULDER
GORGE

GLITTER
BAY

THE
ANCIENT FOREST

OUTER
SPACE

EMERALD GLEN

DEADLY
CREEK

GIANTS' TOWN

RICKETY
BRIDGE

THE
STINKY
SWAMPS

GOLDEN
COVE

Look out for more **bedtime adventures** in

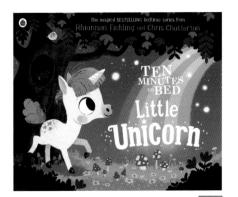

ISBN: 9780241348925 ☐

ISBN: 9780241348918 ☐

ISBN: 9780241372678 ☐

ISBN: 9780241414576 ☐

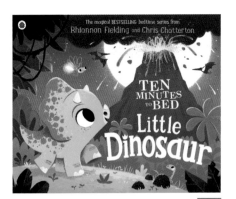

ISBN: 9780241386736 ☐

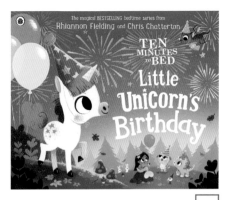

ISBN: 9780241453162 ☐

ISBN: 9780241464373 ☐

ISBN: 9780241464397 ☐

ISBN: 9780241545591 ☑